BUTTERF.

Kristine Ong Muslim is the author of several books of fiction and poetry: *Age of Blight* (Unnamed Press, 2016), *A Roomful of Machines* (ELJ Publications, 2015), *Grim Series* (Popcorn Press, 2012), *We Bury the Landscape* (Queen's Ferry Press, 2012), as well as *Black Arcadia* and *Lifeboat*, two poetry collections from university presses in the Philippines. She also serves as poetry editor of *LONTAR: The Journal of Southeast Asian Speculative Fiction*, a literary journal published by Epigram Books in Singapore, and co-editor (with Nalo Hopkinson) of *Lightspeed Magazine*'s anthology *People of Colo(u)r Destroy Science Fiction*. Widely published in magazines and anthologies, she grew up and continues to live in rural southern Philippines. *Butterfly Dream* is her sixth book.

SNUGGLY BOOKS

kristine ong muslim

butterfly
dream

snuggly slim no. 4

THIS IS A SNUGGLY BOOK

Copyright © 2016 by Kristine Ong Muslim
All rights reserved.

ISBN: 978-1-943813-11-7

Notes and Acknowledgments

Grateful acknowledgment is made to the editors of the following publications in which the early versions of these stories appeared: *Atomjack*, *Cardinal Sins Journal*, *Ellipsis*, *Escape Into Life*, *Fiction Southeast*, *Jupiter SF*, *Labyrinth Inhabitant Magazine*, *One Buck Horror*, *Sein und Werden*, *Southern Pacific Review*, *The Literary Bone*, *The Specusphere*, and *Thursday Never Looking Back: an Anthology for the End of the World* (the Youth & Beauty Brigade, 2012).

The recurring declaration, "This is called the transformation of things," is lifted from a translation of Zhuang Zhou's account of his butterfly dream as put forth by *The Indiana Companion to Traditional Chinese Literature* (edited by William Nienhauser, Jr. and published by the Indiana University Press). Renditions of René Descartes' dream argument and Plato's Forms are also used and misused throughout.

Contents

butterfly
dream

Artificial Life

WE walk into any room, and as expected, we catch Patty trying to bring the doll back to life. She breathes onto the sewn lips that won't ever give up a throat, forces the air into the doll's lungs if it has any, and pauses to imagine the doll's first stirrings of life. But then like always, the doll does not respond to Patty's resuscitation efforts.

Yet, we do not make attempts to stop Patty, even if we know that there is nothing she can do for the doll. We have seen her as a child. We have understood how she is sustained by her love for cogs and fallen machinery, for a seed slowly kicking up earth to make way for its shoots and the initial root displays on an air-grafted portion of a tree, for tiny hatchlings being freed of their shells and other forms of beginnings.

As for the doll—the thing was born dead and will remain dead. Just another addition to a collector's inventory of lovely, undeveloped objects to be coveted off the shelf, bought, and finally relegated to a closet containing others just like it.

But Patty, well, she simply doesn't give up. Every morning, she brings out the doll from the closet, checks its pulse, begins her rote resuscitation, ignores our sneering and our rehearsed version of the realistic confines of life. Oh, how she pays no heed to our advice—that misplaced hope is a bad thing, that patience is not always a virtue, etc. Day after day after day.

The Six Mutations of Jerome

MILES away from my island, there exists a man named Jerome, a man who can be anyone and anything. So, if you have what I have, if you happen to have magic eyes and are willing to look closely enough at the world you inhabit and the world that shall soon wear you down, then you'll see a little bit of what I see. You'll figure out the limits of wakefulness, the rationale behind the dream argument, the crude machinery that drove the butterfly dream. Because out there, the hideous, the disfigured, and the inspired lie awake in bed, the pupils of their magic eyes dilating. They toil all their lives and earn what they want, what they think they want. One of us has to catalogue their exploits. Otherwise, we'd be saddled by this one-sided construction of reality.

So, two hours each night, I look out from the window of my self-appointed, windowless rubber room. Then I write down my observations. I do not know that many big, multi-syllabic words but I have managed to write down most of what I have seen. One by one, I describe and give names to all the graceful mutations, the ordinariness of sounds, smells, textures, wants. Then I become less alone. This is called the transformation of things. . . .

You know Jerome as Hanged Man, who took the fall and hung himself from the trellis next to his porch. He was the one who never really went away. His neighbor saw his dangling form and called the police. His body was driven away, cremated, but he then stayed. A knotted blue cord around the neck. Suspended right there at the same spot where bougainvilleas cannot grow. Suspended but not swaying because the wind was not strong enough to give him any semblance of movement.

Hanged Man's first death was uncomplicated and followed the natural mechanism—a few moments for brain activity to cease and then approximately fifteen to twenty minutes for the rest of the body to follow. The second death took an eternity because he never really went away like the others before him.

When Hanged Man was still alive, he spent a lot of time fighting the urge to kill himself. He tried all sorts of drugs and all manners of questionable therapy, but nothing worked. Did Hanged Man think that what he had was a sickness of the spirit? Did he will himself to stay alive all those years because the spirit—for all its metaphysical fluff—was the same as will? Do you know that his dog died of grief a few days after he killed himself?

During dry and windy days, air moved in and out of Hanged Man's slightly opened mouth, slithering—*I am your song, I am your song, I am your song*—exorcising what ravages the body, the body that was no longer there, the body that was never really there.

At some point, you will be convinced that Hanged Man can see you in color, see everyone in color even through the blindness that came with physical death. Suspended there in his porch. Staying there. A knotted blue nylon cord around the neck. Framed by the trellis where bougainvilleas cannot grow. Very still now. Very still.

Jerome as Kettle Man

You know Jerome as Kettle Man, who lives inside the kettle. He hisses from his burning stand. His steel bottoms slightly redden. His pointed snout whistles. His snout is as pointed as the steeple of a church with doors just wide enough to accommodate the sins of one man. Just one man. And that, for you, is enough.

You whisper, "Please," when you take his water. Kettle Man is not used to being treated with anything resembling respect. The new experience unnerves him. As a result, his water has a slightly bitter metallic taste to it.

You know what he is ultimately responsible for—*silence*. When Kettle Man was eight, he walked into his parents' bedroom at the most inopportune time. The moment he turned the doorknob, a loud bang shattered the silence of their idyllic two-storey house. When the door was fully opened, he saw his father slumped on the floor. His blood was a red map across the beige headboard. Kettle Man remembered the lopsided arm of the bedside lamp. Kettle Man remembered the blue travel guide to Poland next to the bedside lamp. Kettle Man remembered the white rug on the floor stained by blood spots the size of pennies.

Kettle Man's mother rushed into the room. She was wearing perfume although she was supposed to have been working in the kitchen. She smelled of gardenias and something else, something musky underneath the cloying floral scent. Years later, Kettle Man would learn that the musky undertone was the distinctive odor of ambergris. Her eyes darted in panic to find the young Kettle Man inside the room. She did not react when she saw her husband's slumped body on the bed. She was only scared because her son was inside the room. "You're supposed to be asleep," she said. Then she was crying. She did not stop crying until the police arrived and took the fallen body away.

The police said that there was no foul play. Kettle Man did not tell anyone about what he thought truly happened to his father. Thinking of that moment years later, Kettle Man was sure that what he heard was not a bang but a muffled pop. It did not even sound fatal.

So, all his life he makes up for the silence. He has been whistling, screaming, hissing, throwing fits—again and again his water abandoning him, escaping as steam.

Jerome as Stick Man

You know Jerome as Stick Man, who lives inside the matchbox. He was always afraid of splintering, of breaking, of questioning how far he could bend to reach his nonexistent feet. You tried to light his blackened bulb of a head, and he recoiled, exposed himself in colors—blue in the middle, yellow in the flame radiating outwards of what appeared as his fragile wick.

When Stick Man was five, he discovered he had a sister. His sister happened to be the filthy eight year old whom his mother placed inside the closet for many years until one day the police came into the house and took his mother and his sister away. He lived with his aunt until he turned eighteen.

He tried to find his sister but did not exert much of an effort. Instead, he made one half-hearted attempt merely out of curiosity. He began and ended the search for his sister behind a social worker's desk.

Stick Man, who had been Jerome, shook the social worker's hand before leaving the room. And, if you had been an outsider looking in, it would have looked to you that Stick Man was holding the social worker's mouth open to get the truth out of her. Holding her mouth open, seeing what was inside her throat, expecting something or someone to come out.

The social worker did not even give Stick Man his sister's name, which was Lauren.

Jerome as Multiple Personality Disorder

You know Jerome as Jerome, who is fragmented. Because he is fragmented, he is convinced he is whole. He asks to be left alone many times each day, but Carl, the old man inside him, endlessly nags him to mind his manners, to chew with his mouth closed, to not call just about any woman a "bitch," and to say "please" when asking for something.

Back when he still had to go to work, had no choice but to talk to people, and had errands that forced him to step outside the house, he never opened his mouth wide enough for fear that the old man inside him would end up escaping. He could feel Carl excitedly scramble for a foothold along the slippery sides of his throat. Jerome swallowed fast to keep Carl back down where bile and stomach acids churned. Jerome did not know what would happen if Carl got out, but it scared him nonetheless.

Gene was the youngest, the angriest of them all. But he had not grown any hands yet so he could not do serious damage. Gene gave them all—him, Carl, and the silent one, Matthew—several bad dreams, the kind that made them wet the bed. Strange how the dreams never unfolded in color; the dream scenes were always rendered in black and white.

At some point, you finally notice that Jerome finds that the therapist is a bore; she kept asking him how many windows he had in his childhood home. To indulge her and to keep her talking, Jerome said that there were five windows in all. Of course, he did not include the crack in the kitchen wall where he had spied on his mother the day she measured out poison into his father's soup.

Gene insisted that there were only two windows, while Matthew, the quiet one, declared that there were no windows at all. He said that he grew up in a room that was always dark, possibly windowless. He was also the one who implanted the idea that whenever you emptied yourself, parts of you might grow weak and fracture in some places. Something else might slip in between the cracks. Then one summer, something did slip in. *Gene.*

"Can we talk to Matthew?" the doctor asked.

"He's busy, Doc." Jerome said in a guttural drawl that sounded like one made by an animal responding to the faraway mating call of its pack.

"Do you know where he is right now, Jerome?"

"Matthew was here when you weren't looking. You never look in the right places."

The doctor did not react.

Jerome coughed and gagged as if he were choking. "Shit, it's Carl." He recovered his composure after a few minutes. Red-faced, he said, "He never gives up. I hate that old man."

Silently and without looking at him in the eye, she switched off her portable recorder and walked out of the room. She was tired, hungry, looking forward to a nice quiet evening at home.

An orderly entered the room and wheeled Jerome away. No one noticed the tiny hand emerge from Jerome's mouth. The back of the palm was wrinkled and the skin was marred with liver spots—noticeable against the backdrop of pale skin. The liver spots and wrinkled skin brought to mind the hands of someone who was very, very old.

Jerome as Elizabeth

You know Jerome as Jerome, who prefers to be called Elizabeth. Jerome's handlers made it sound like a disease—her insistence on being called Elizabeth—but you knew it for what it was—a miracle. What Elizabeth had was a miracle.

Eleven and a half years ago, you heard that she was diagnosed by almost all—whether they were equipped to do so or not—the people she loved. She was diagnosed to suffer from Seymour's Eyes, which can be misconstrued as a set of psychosomatic symptoms that start off without warning in the form of a twitching sensation around the eye area. The twitching lasts overnight. When a person who has it wakes up from it, he sees things differently. Jerome, who is also Elizabeth, woke up from it knowing exactly what she wanted, what she needed, how to go about securing what she needed. It is highly likely that Jerome does not know yet how to get what she wants, but you might consider that as a minor trade off.

Seymour's Eyes, like all miracles, leave souvenirs in their wake. The only way to miss out on the souvenirs is to not pay attention. As for Jerome, who is also Elizabeth, he was left with the *animals*.

Elizabeth's animals have neither fur nor feathers. They sit in one corner of her house, waiting to be fed. There is no possible way to beckon out to them. They make the decision whether or not to approach the person who owns them. They have malformed eyes, and they cannot hear very well, but they observe and understand what goes on before them—you know that Elizabeth knows this because her animals once pounced on one of her dinner guests. During the ensuing scuffle, it was revealed that the guest had surreptitiously pocketed two pieces of her fine heirloom silverware. Elizabeth's animals also possess disproportionately large tongues. Their wide tongues are not the sort of tongues which one would expect to use for lapping up leftovers. Those tongues are designed to take, take, take—more than what is given—like most people you know.

Elizabeth's animals do not need her. It is the other way around. This is called the transformation of things. Isolation is something that she truly fears even more than, say, being rejected. One time, Elizabeth broke down at work, embarrassing herself in front of two of her superiors. It suddenly hit her that when she got home, she would discover that her animals had vanished. Finding that corner of the house empty was her worst fear. So, she rushed home in the middle of the workday. Thankfully, she found her animals still intact, their oversized tongues still repugnant in their self-appointed places.

How you wish you can say more, but life just does not work that way. There are many stories that are not supposed to be told. Not because they have nothing new to say, but because they were designed to unfold in their own time. Like the back story, for example, behind why her name is Elizabeth even if everybody calls her Jerome.

Jerome as Burned Man

You know Jerome as Burned Man, who will someday heal. He was once the man inside the burning house, the man who died one minute and twenty-six seconds before the first fireman arrived to put out the flames. You had nothing to do with his death, but somehow you felt responsible. That is how you generally feel when good men die.

The fire was an accident, according to the news. You never met Burned Man when he was alive. His wife owned a small gallery, and she once hired you as a back-room worker. From several news stories you pieced together Burned Man's history: married, no kids, self-made millionaire at thirty-two. He gave money to several charities and strangely did not drive a fancy car. He was also described as having complete heterochromia. The iris of his left eye was bluish; the other was greenish.

Two weeks after he was cremated, Burned Man appeared in the burn unit of the Station Tower General Hospital. Two nurses quit working because they kept seeing Burned Man lying on a gurney or sitting on a bench—just sitting there, probably waiting for his turn to get a skin graft or a new lease on life. Then he vanished after a few seconds, only to reappear the next day—skin peeling, some patches of burnt skin plopping on to the floor, determination in his eyes—the bluish eye on the left and the greenish one on the right.

One of the nurses who saw him was a close friend of yours. She told you about the odd eye color. It was Burned Man, all right, and he wanted to be saved and somehow brought back to life.

You hope he can still be helped. Consider how his scorched skin is shedding away, revealing raw flesh underneath—you believe he is healing from the inside. He may soon come back, alive and well. This is called the transformation of things.

In the Eye of the Beholder

TWO weeks after Jimmy's mother died in the hospital, he could still see her looking down at him from the top of the stairs. Her eyes were wide and bloodshot. Her tongue, blackened. In her breath was the smell of cigarettes and desperation. Her lips were parched and frozen into a scream like an upturned and bottomless black coffee cup the rim of which was riddled with bees.

"Please, Mom," Jimmy said for the third time that day, "go away." He looked straight at her, trying hard not to throw up. Even from a distance, he could smell her rancid cigarette breath. He only wanted to collect the dragon kite in his room and take it outside, yet there she was again, marring everything with her presence.

He heard his father tinkering under the sink in the kitchen. The sound of the neighbor's twin kids playing in the inflatable backyard pool made him want to scream. They did not have any right to be happy.

The ghost of his mother at the head of the stairs droned on and on, "Why, baby . . . why . . . ?" She said it over and over until Jimmy could not take it anymore. He slammed the front door, fled to the porch.

❋

Jimmy was seven years old when he first met his loud-mouthed cousin Marty, who was home from the summer camp. That was the time Jimmy first considered leaping off the terrace to the paved driveway below.

"Maybe, it will go away," Marty told him, trying hard not to wince at Jimmy's enucleated left eye socket. "Maybe, it will grow back. Then you'll have a new eye."

Aunt Terrie took Marty away. Jimmy heard her talking to Marty in the living room, but he could not make out the words.

Being born with one eye missing had never bothered Jimmy until Marty pointed out to him that something was wrong with not having a left eye. His father always said that it was because he was "special," and special people did not care about what non-special people thought. But Jimmy did not want to be special. He only wanted to look like everyone else. Like Marty. Marty had friends, and Marty could watch the parade and take his roller blades to the park. Marty had a left eye.

That night, with Aunt Terrie and her son sleeping in the guest room across the hall, Jimmy dreamed of white worms coming out of his hollow left eye socket. It itched when the worms slithered in and out. He woke up, feverish and stifling his screams. He did not want to hear anyone say that it was only a dream. He did not want anyone to comfort or pity him. They always lied to him about how they understood his feelings. No one would ever understand how he felt.

On the day his mother was supposed to go home—cured again—from the hospital, eleven-year-old Jimmy left his favorite toy car on the stairs. *Mom and Dad,* Jimmy thought, *it did not matter who. I hate them.* Luck, it seemed, and the toy did not have a chance because his mother failed to come home. He would surprise his father one of these days with rat poison in his beer.

Toy car.

Jimmy forgot about the wailing ghost and his dragon kite. He thought harder. He remembered rushing to the phone in the hallway. He remembered the afternoon light filtered by the blinds so that it appeared as streaks across the floor, streaks of thin, equally spaced lines. He remembered hearing Snowy, the neighbor's dog, barking outside. He remembered the sound of the ringing phone and going downstairs to answer it. His footfalls on the wood parquet floor were loud in the empty house.

His father emerged from the kitchen doorway. He did not even look at Jimmy. He went straight upstairs and embraced his mother. "Please, Geena, he's dead," Jimmy's father said. "We can't go on like this. You know it was an accident."

This time, Jimmy did not try to hold back his screams. And just like before, nobody heard him.

The Girl Who Did Not Exist

INSISTED to the bald man that there was no Lauren, but he wouldn't stop asking me about her. It looked as if he only wanted to hear me say her name, like it was very important that I admit to him that the girl the police found in the empty closet under the stairs was real.

I said, "No, you can't make me. There is no Lauren. There is no Lauren. There is no Lauren. That closet has nothing in it, because Mommy said that there are rats. We can't put anything in a room with rats. The rats eat everything."

The fat woman kept on stroking the small of my back. She wore a blue ID with a logo that said something about social services. She was the only person I liked. She had given me a doughnut earlier. It was the special one in the box. It was the doughnut sprinkled with confetti. Blue and red confetti.

The bald man got excited when someone peeked in to say that "we have the neighbor." I was happy to see him go out of the room.

The fat woman asked me about "Lauren." She was kind, so I had to, at least, give her something back.

"I didn't know she was supposed to be called Lauren," I said. That was the truth. "When the police led her out of the closet—that's the first time I've seen her. I have no sister. And she doesn't look too good, so she cannot be my sister."

She smiled. "Well, have you ever seen Marcus open the closet door under the stairs?"

"Uhm, no. I'm sure Mom will ask him to move out of the house soon. She gets tired of all her boyfriends."

"So, there were other boyfriends before Marcus?" I noticed how her eyes lit up. I knew she was probably onto something because she hid her look of interest immediately.

"Yep."

"Can you tell me about them?"

"Jack had a tattoo of an owl. He said that when you poke the owl's eyes at midnight, you release the magic and all your wishes come true. I think Jack was lying."

She scribbled something. "Oh, that's amazing. I'm pretty sure the owl does not appreciate being poked, magic or not. Anyway, when did you last see Jack?"

We talked for what seemed like hours. She probably liked kids because she made a funny expression, sort of like anger held back, when I told her how Marcus once went inside my room while I was changing into my pajamas. She did not write it down.

I expected her to ask me if Marcus "touched" me, but she didn't. Perhaps, that would come later. That's how they did it in the cop shows that Gramps used to watch. I miss Gramps. He used to read me *The Ballad of Stick Man*.

That afternoon, a gloved woman in the hospital prodded and inspected me down there. Hated it. I got the cramps spreading my legs so she could go about her business, telling me over and over, "Relax, Jenny, this will be over soon."

She let me rest in my hospital bed. It was all white there, and looked so clean. They let me watch cartoons, too. I was feeling sleepy when I noticed that the nurse forgot the remote control on the chair near the bedside table. I took it, changed the channel, watched a toothpaste commercial. Then I saw our house! On television! A guy was saying something about a girl locked in a closet for ten years. I couldn't understand the rest of what he was saying. He was talking about the girl, Lauren, who was supposed to be my sister. But there was no Lauren. Why couldn't they get it? There was no girl in the closet. Maybe, the police simply put the girl in there.

I changed the channel. Oh, the chipmunks can sing!

Wreck, Slash, Burn

BLIP was part ice, and he melted with the ferocity of an elephant in heat. Nobody in the group wanted to touch him lest he complain again about the peculiar itchiness of slow melting. It was finally agreed upon that no one, not even Blip himself, could touch Blip's sacrosanct iciness.

The room was quiet until Bungy spoke. The infrared logo, which was embedded on his forehead, glowed when he opened his mouth. "We have to think of something to talk about," he grumbled with the sullen idiotic expression of a 3D-printed android.

"Affirmative," agreed the butt-faced Banderpansy.

"Will the Master approve of us talking?" said the blushing Bio, a subservient toilet cleaner.

"The Master is asleep, you dumbass!" Blip cut in. A trickle of moisture on his face followed this outburst. "We have been working all day. I think it's only humanly that the Master will, at the very least, allow us to talk. Or humans are just being humans these days."

"Affirmative," Banderpansy approved again.

Bungy said: "I miss my mother."

"But you don't have a mother, Bungy. You are only a soulless, slightly sentient little bugger with nothing to do except to sort the mail," replied Blip. "You don't need a mother for that."

"I guess I just miss my nonexistent mother, that's all."

"Affirmative." Banderpansy again.

"Humans have mothers," Bio said proudly. "The Master has one."

"Does it matter, you bootlicking, crap-eating, smelly idiot?" Blip regarded him furiously, marveling at Bio's moronic devotion to the Master. "It's the fate of their diseased evolution. They have to be nursed first in their mother's wombs. Then they have to be delivered with forceps and doctors and nurses. Isn't it cute how helpless they can become?"

"Affirmative," said Banderpansy.

Bungy was getting edgy this time. This talk of blasphemy against the Master was worrying him. "Maybe we should just bleep off?"

"Affirmative." Banderpansy seconded.

'I don't care if humans are not self-sustaining," Bio was adamant, a toilet cleaner who wipes the butt of his master everyday. "The Master is still the master."

Blip, enraged with the toilet cleaner, was slowly melting now. Small drops of water created a pool around his stainless steel stand. "Your mother was supposed to be made out of dung, Bio, didn't it ever occur to you? But they carted her off because the planet was too full of dung, and they didn't need other dung to fill the space for more dung." Blip put it in nicely, his infrared eyes scanning with anger.

"Thank you," Bio said politely. He was too dumb to understand the sarcasm. Well, he was only a near-obsolete model of a toilet cleaner.

"Why would a machine need a mother anyway?" Bungy muttered to no one in particular, wondering.

"Affirmative."

"I think you only need a little calibration, Bungy," Blip said. "When machines talk metaphysics, it means that their logic circuits are a little blumpy."

"The Master never needs to be calibrated," Bio said triumphantly. "He takes a crap and pisses without any pre-programming arrangement."

"Forget it!" Blip was getting closer to murder this time.

"Affirmative," Banderpansy agreed.

The Lonely People

Nobody Is Watching

AFTER twenty-six years, the first family of fugitives finally found the weakest part of the barrier. It was Margaret, not the pyrokinetic Eddie, who first discovered the worn coating underneath the bioluminescent blue-green foliage. She prodded it with her nails. The insulation budged. It would not do that under normal circumstances. She excitedly clawed at the PVC wires lining the layer of insulation, tripping the alarms at the Station. But it did not matter to her. Before the guards could get there, they would all be on the other side.

Father called out to the apparition that he claimed was named Jack, the son—*his* son—who had never been born. "Please don't go, Jack—we're almost free," he implored, talking to no one beyond the trees and the parasite-laden jungle. "Come back here."

Eddie told him to forget about Jack. But it was no use. Father stubbornly followed the path which his nonexistent son supposedly took, leading him away from where they could extricate themselves from that dark world and the Station. Eddie was about to run to get him.

"Stay with me, Ed," she said. "Let Father go. Help me get these wires off."

He debated whether to save Father or to save himself. Common sense won, and he wildly scratched and pulled at the membranous material of the barrier's insulation.

"Hurry, Ed."

"What about Father?"

She said with no trace of remorse: "He'll die soon enough anyway, whether we get to the other side or not. Do you see the veins protruding in his left arm? That's where the parasites got him. He would not last for another month."

When the hole was wide enough to pass through, she went in first.

It was a roadside. She could see from afar what looked like a diner, a gasoline station, and a smattering of houses. Tracts of farmlands lay ahead. The neon lights of the diner would not be switched on until after five more hours had passed. A road sign proclaimed the location: *Outerbridge, Mile 19.*

She had recognized a similar setting from the films they had been replaying when they could not sleep at the Station. The sun was high up in the sky. She had never been outside in the open whenever the sun was up. Back at the Station, they were conditioned to stay indoors and to go out only when it was dark.

Margaret whistled to signal at the grisly, salivating creature in the corner, the creature that pretended to be a dog. It leaped through the ragged hole, severed its left earlobe cleanly when it snagged the wires. It yelped in pain beside her. Eddie slinked through and immediately approached the injured family pet. He pacified it by stroking its fur. It reacted like any normal dog would—it wagged its tail and settled down beside Eddie. Margaret quickly shorted the wires to seal the barrier opening.

Eddie gagged and spat. The vegetation where his saliva landed had wilted away. "What's that smell?"

"It's air—nitrogen, oxygen, and some inert traces," she said. "You're smelling pollen. It's springtime. Better get used to it."

Eddie recovered after a few minutes. He admired the way Margaret took in that new world. She acted as if she were born to be a part of that place. "So, where to?" he asked.

"It's very big out there." She smiled. "We can go just about anywhere."

A mile or so from the road, a woman shielded her eyes to make out the three approaching forms. She thought that there was something wrong, something disjointed about the way they walked.

Abstractions on a Sky Called Arthur

Like most people in this world, Arthur was disfigured, but he made up for it by his lack of eyes.

"It is blue Arthur," his mother told him when he decided to gouge out his eyes so he could no longer be fooled. "The sky has always been blue. *They* forgot to change it into something we couldn't recognize. For me, I think it's a curse that it's remained that way. It reminds me of everything else that has been changed."

"I don't care, Mother. You can go on and see whatever is pulled right in front of your eyes, but me, well—

I'm free, am I not? They can no longer influence me with those stupid colorful skins, shapeshifting walls for autosuggestion, molting rainbows, disgusting pink stars to make us believe in miracles."

"You sound just like your father before they got him. I can keep you safe here, as long as you don't try to go out."

"Go out to *see* what, Mother?"

"You're too young to remember what we did to this planet, Arthur," she said. "After the war, there was nothing left for the survivors to reconstruct. Until they came and taught us contentment, that what we see makes us covet things. They changed everything that was wrong about this planet——"

"Shut up, Mother. I'm sick of it. I hear that version of history all the time on TV."

"You're just tired, Arthur. The bleeding has stopped. That's good. I think we should have dinner now." She headed to the doorway and left Arthur to clean up the dried blood on his face and hands. The doorway accommodated her and loosened up its membranous hinges a bit so she could pass.

Abstractions on a World Called Shirley

The box was small, small enough to fit in the curve of her left palm. Her right one had dissolved a long time ago. It was hard to believe that a box that small could mean something. Shirley wished for it to contain a gift. If not a gift, then perhaps something special to compensate for the shadow that she had to give up in order to earn a room in the Shelter.

She heard the gurgling of the giant mechanical worm outside the building. She tried to be afraid only to feel normal again, but she was too tired to even bother conjuring the right fear reflexes. There would be time for that later.

She glanced at the tongue-bed; it was damp and marred with pores from all the things it had lapped before. Although it looked safe because it was still asleep, its edges had ulcerations. Easing carefully on the tongue-bed so as not to wake it prematurely, Shirley puzzled over the tiny box she had found two world-hours ago inside the shed. The box had no visible flaps. It was nearly weightless, smooth, and durable. Was it meant to be opened like all the other boxes before it?

They will get you someday, her brother, Arthur, said to her when she opened the doorway and never looked back. That was the time Shirley lost her right hand; the doorway had to take something. The last words she heard before she disappeared with her dreams of escape were the screams of her little sister, Mischa: "Only five stitches, Shirley. Five stitches to close the mouth of the Apocalypse. . . ."

The landscape in and out of the doorway was tainted from end to end. Only the sky was left intact. It was still blue with fluffs of very real-looking white clouds ensconced in certain areas. Her mother said that they had forgotten to change the sky. Did it matter—what was left unchanged? Shirley did not think so. She only hoped that she could still find a way to warn her siblings.

Outside, the giant mechanical worm was still producing the same sloshing sound. It was making its rounds to catch stray people, knowing that the carnivorous Shelter was impregnable and kept all of its guests behind its membranous hinges. Behind the door, the clock was ticking. The walls had little human arms that waved to and fro in a motion that was both mesmerizing and annoying. There were no piles of bones on the floor, which was a good sign. The room was not hungry yet. There would be time for that later. Shirley, after twenty-five years of running, discovered that she no longer cared and went to sleep.

Abstractions on a Window Called Mischa

Something happened one day that made Mischa build her own window out of leaves (the real ones cast down by real trees), powdered macroscopic dust mites as adhesive, glass, and silicon wood for the pane. The window was big enough so she could ease her head out to look at the gnarled feet of the building where the tourists had been eaten two days ago. Mischa could have built a larger one, but natural laws dictated otherwise. The window that she built with her hands alone made her feel free. Now, she could see all the metallic birds outside—their wings silvery, their feathers ruffled to simulate the effects of moving air, their beaks curving into arcs of light. And the sky—still blue. The sky was the only thing that was left unchanged.

Through her window, she could observe the giant mechanical worm nuzzling all the dark places where survivors might hide. From a distance, the worm did not look dangerous anymore.

The floor pulsed and gurgled softly underneath her. Somehow, there was no way to ignore it. She tried not to wince lest the floor could smell her anxiety and growing fear. There was no way to predict what floors might do in that situation.

She wondered what had happened to her sister Shirley, the first one to enter the doorway. That was the time Shirley had lost her right hand; the doorway had to take something. But Mischa knew that Shirley was a survivor, and she would most likely end up inside one of the rooms in the Shelter. Determined to find her sister, she hurried to assemble the window. She fixed shard after shard into place. The window would claim her left eye, like all windows would, but it would be worth it. The right eye was enough to guide her. If only Shirley were still alive . . .

The next day, intent on escaping, Mischa unraveled the window just big enough for her body to fit in and small enough to fold and hide in her pressed lips.

Abstractions on a Drain Called Emmett

Emmett's fingertips tested the circumference of the drain-hole. *It would hold.* There was supposed to be a seam there somewhere. A breach that opens to the other side, like the doorway that took the hand of his cousin Shirley.

All doorways had to take something. It would be worth it. Shirley had told him the day before she disappeared.

The P-trap shook. A segment of the giant mechanical worm was caught in it. The worm segment was harmless as long as it remained in the dark. The light made it grow robust and predatory.

The floor underneath him was the only problem. It would grow hungry soon. A wet gurgling sound from the nails that hammered the floorboards into place was the first sign. And he had heard it one a minute before. Emmett saw bone dust in the crevices between the floorboards. Remnants of the unlucky ones who had no reason to stand on the floor when it was hungry.

The seam! He had to find it. The drain was not yielding to his touch. Maybe, it was only a myth. Although nobody from the other side ever came back to prove that there was, indeed, a seam around the circumference of the drain, Shirley was never wrong about things.

Using the properties of the drain would not result in pain, but it might not lead to the other side. But we have no choice, Emmett. You've got to find the seam. There has to be one. I'll use the doorway.

Emmett hoped that Shirley was still alive. Shirley was a survivor; she knew the streets and had a feel for the restlessness of the breathing rooms better than anyone else in the clan. She also pointed out to him that the sky was still left unchanged, that they had forgotten to change it. Perhaps, there were other things that were unchanged as well. From these unchanged things, the original world could be reconstructed.

His thumb began to blister as it brushed against the hairless skin of the sink. This same surface was where he had watched his grandparents get sucked in. *Stop thinking about it,* he thought. *Find the goddamn seam.*

For the first time, he became aware of the stillness of the room. Something was clearly amiss. The room was no longer breathing.

Now where are the seams? The conventional axis for a revolving cylinder passed through the hollow core parallel to the five stitches to close the mouth of the Apocalypse and all the doors gave up their meanings when left open much longer than necessary and the windows were upright slabs of all that were cold and fleeting and the blanket on the cot would never be thick enough against it. Think. Think. Where are the seams?

Another gurgling sound from the floor underneath. He looked down to check if a mouth was forming. That's when he noticed a projection on the floor. The mouth! He averted his gaze, tried to calm down, concentrated on finding the seam. When he looked at the drain again, Emmett caught a glimpse of his dissolving thumb. It did not hurt at all. He did not understand how he could use the drain as a doorway when he did not even know where the seam was located or what it looked like. His whole arm disappeared down the drain. He felt air against his disappearing arm. *There was something down there. Maybe this was the way that Shirley was talking about.*

The upper lip of the floor edged up closer to his left shoe. Emmett grasped the lining of the drain. He was surprised to find that it had grown soft, and he could now stretch the drain opening wide enough to fit his body. He was twisting his torso down the blackness of the drain when the mouth of the floor nipped at his left foot. The shoe and two of his digits came off. No pain.

There was a circle of light farther ahead. The end of the drain-hole?

Emmett hoped to see Shirley on the other side.

Abstractions on a House Called Jack

Here is the godforsaken house. We wait for the doors to open.

Mother, the one on the picture and the one who smiled with her eyes closed, used to tell us that the floor was the most important part of any house. "You can have a leaky faucet or a creaky door, but not loose floorboards or bad carpeting," she would say. None of my brothers understood the logic behind it. But we believed her just the same.

The machines had come and gone, the doors swinging open behind them, and we stayed wide-eyed awaiting their inevitable return. Tap water drummed against the stainless steel sink. Every dull trickle created its own rhythm.

Inside the busted water pipes, the mechanical dust mites scurried about their little feet, dragging the years behind them and the drone of their pointless lives. Dorian had tried to shut them up many years before using a polarizer. The mites had always returned, always appearing on the left side of the wall. Emmett, my eldest brother, said to just let the mechanical dust mites be. "They've been on this planet before the dinosaurs," he said. "They deserve a little respect for surviving that long."

Under the stairs, the spinning room toiled to keep the house going. What does it see—that thing inside the spinning room, that thing with no eyes? I imagined the valves hissing to keep up with the carbon dioxide we exhaled.

Meanwhile, Dorian found a happiness bottle inside the cupboards. It was nestled among the beer bottles, and jars of gourmet pickles. One squirt from the happiness bottle, and we were all froth from head to toe—part darkness, part hope. The side effects were bearable— blurred vision, tinnitus, and palpitations. Occasionally, we hear voices in our head.

"Tell us where you keep the books," Father intoned in some faraway afterlife. We could smell the cigarette on his breath, taste his rancid sweat.

"Leave the boys alone," Mother answered. "Just leave them alone, Chuck. They would learn the rules later. They would realize that they could not do anything about all these."

Dorian laughed himself to tears. Emmett hummed the tune of a commercial for spicy ramen. As for me, I took in my happiness silently.

Something, someone pulled open the back door. We heard the rattling as the door hinges were torn off from the wall, but we were too drunk with happiness to even care.

Letter to a Certain Dr. Bill

D EAR DR. BILL,

I received your message. I meant to call you back yesterday but did not want to talk to you over the phone. I'll see you on Monday. I promise to show up at 8:00.

I still think about what you told me during one of our non-billable sessions when you allowed me to rant. I never told you that I already bought a wife, one of the first-rate Loyals. Two months ago, she was home-delivered to me by a dealer in Cambodia. Oh, Doc, you should have seen the dude—a dreadlocked guy who sells all types of black-market merchandise, from pristine Tang Dynasty porcelain jars to Sarcosuchus imperator fossils. As for my wife, she cost $600 dollars per month. That cost does not include the solar cell upkeep and the synthetic collagen. It's impractical, I know, but this is Outerbridge, the only place in America where crops are still grown in soil.

A long time ago, I went out with this girl. I never forgot what she told me before she asked to be listed as a no-resuscitate. She said: "Sadness is something that you just bottle up, Jack, because it doesn't really last. It's a crippling thing to have, but its hold on you eventually wears off. How long it takes for the sadness to wane varies from one person to another. Some get over it in a day. Some take a lifetime or two to recover. But the most important thing is that sadness doesn't last. Loneliness, well, that's a different ballgame altogether. You only get lonely by choice." *Wise girl.* Too bad she wanted no part of eternal life and opted to sign up for the no-resuscitate program.

--MESSAGE UNREADABLE AND TRUNCATED--
MACHINE-STAMPED AND AUTHENTICATED
TO THIS POINT

I still clean mirrors around the house, Dr. Bill. Every single one of them has been weakened by constant polishing.

--MESSAGE UNREADABLE AND TRUNCATED--
MACHINE-STAMPED AND AUTHENTICATED
TO THIS POINT

What I have may just be a matter of longing. This policy of eternal life has screwed up everything. You know about longing, don't you? Its name is Susan. This Susan waits for the roaches that she alone can see. Susan appears invisible to the roaches. Its name can also be Stephen. Stephen is now serving time in the Bardenstan County Jail. He once dismantled his wife, saw nothing inside her but dried leaves. He was still raking the leaves when the police got to him.

--MESSAGE UNREADABLE AND TRUNCATED--
MACHINE-STAMPED AND AUTHENTICATED
TO THIS POINT

The house would not eat even if I force-fed Lincoln into its basement-mouth. It pretended to be full by belching hair and an occasional fingernail out of the kitchen drain.

Nothing works, Dr, Bill. The drugs you gave me—they only make me groggy. I mistook my wife for an ironing board and accidentally burned her to death.

I also found rats under the floorboards. Yes, rats in the twenty-third century. Imagine that. They shrieked when cornered, just like real rats.

--MESSAGE UNREADABLE AND TRUNCATED--
MACHINE-STAMPED AND AUTHENTICATED
TO THIS POINT

I only wished that you had given me something stronger so I could sleep well.

This cold ends in the body least touched.

Thank you for trying. I'll see you on Monday.

All my best,
Jack

--END OF MESSAGE--
DO NOT BEND
PROPERTY OF
THE OUTERBRIDGE HISTORICAL
RESTORATION TEAM

The Psychopomps

WE drove as far as our bus's limited fuel could take us. This time, my comrade Jackal was the designated driver. Running on fumes and eventually conking out, our yellow bus—or whatever guise our vehicle had taken that time—managed to take us closer to our destination. We herded our respective wards from the backseat, all ninety-two of them, no longer flailing as they were busily growing accustomed to their new forms, their new forms that were at last deprived of a physical body and saddled with pure consciousness, a transformation that had taken the fight out of everyone.

The clearing was as wide and as windy as the last time we delivered our latest haul. The surrounding vegetation, being all plastic, did not rustle in the wind. The illusion of trees in the background was still convincing. The ground, its underside bolstered by lifetimes upon lifetimes of excess baggage that had to be shed off at this point in the journey, was unyielding, steady, unnaturally leveled throughout.

"Is this it?" one of them asked. It was the bearded forty-two-year-old man collected from the gleaming metropolis of Abu Dhabi. He was the last one to emerge from the backseat, the one who, for many years, fancied himself a creative type, a tortured poet, so he churned out banalities and spouted off rehashed Kierkegaard quotes as if they were his own.

"Oh, no!" one of us saw fit to reply. "We still have a long way to go. But we walk from hereon, past the fake trees in the distance to the mirage at the end of the clearing. There shall be a lake there somewhere. It's where you're supposed to wash yourselves clean."

"Clean of what?"

"Clean of—of what you are."

"Ha, this is all a dream," a dark-haired lady chimed in. "I'm going to wake up any minute now."

Jackal laughed hard and snorted in disgust, "Dream on, lady."

"Come on," I said to our latest herd of ninety-two. "Start walking. This is going to be a long day."

And it was, just like before, but not for long.

Milton Keynes UK
Ingram Content Group UK Ltd.
UKHW041445171023
430776UK00004B/507

9 781943 813117